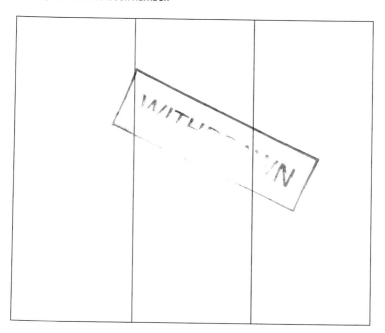

Published by Evans Brothers Limited
2A Portman Mansions
Chiltern Street
London W1U 6NR

© Evans Brothers Limited 2009

Printed in China

British Library Cataloguing in Publication data

Francis, Pauline.
  David Copperfield. -- (Fast track classics)
  1. Orphans--Juvenile fiction. 2. Children's stories.
  3. Bildungsromans.
  I. Title II. Series III. Dickens, Charles, 1812-1870.
  823.9'2-dc22

ISBN-13: 9780237539092

DAVID COPPERFIELD

Introduction

Charles Dickens was born in 1812, the second of eight children. When he was twelve years old, his father went to prison because he owed money. Charles went out to work to help his family. He never forgot this terrible time when he was poor, and later used his experiences in some of his stories.

In his twenties, Charles found work writing about London life for newspapers and magazines. Some of these articles were published as a book called *The Pickwick Papers*. This is how Charles Dickens became famous at the age of twenty-four.

David Copperfield was published as a novel in 1850. It tells the story of a young boy called David who, after his mother's death, has to find his own way in a harsh world – and who dreams of becoming a writer. He makes many friends on the way, both good and bad.

Charles Dickens wrote many famous novels, including *Nicholas Nickleby*, *A Christmas Carol*, *Oliver Twist* and *Great Expectations*. He died in 1870 at the age of fifty-eight and is buried in Westminster Abbey, London.

CHAPTER ONE

Unwanted

I only had one relation in the world, apart from my dear mother. She was my dead father's aunt, Miss Betsey Trotwood. She did not approve of my father's marriage, because she thought that my mother was young and foolish. But after my father's death, she came to visit my mother, who was expecting a child.

'The baby will be a girl,' she declared.

'But it might be a boy,' my mother said.

'Nonsense, it *must* be a girl,' Miss Trotwood replied.

But I was that baby, named David Copperfield after my father. And Miss Betsey Trotwood left our house on the day that I was born – never to return.

Such was the story that my mother's servant, Miss Peggotty, loved to tell me as I was growing up.

My mother, Miss Peggotty and I were very happy together in our little house in Suffolk. Then, one day, a gentleman rang the doorbell. I recognised him, for he had walked home from church with us the Sunday before. His name was Mr Murdstone. I didn't like him, or his deep voice. I was jealous.

One day, Peggotty asked me if I would like to visit the town of Yarmouth with her.

'My brother, Mr Peggotty, lives there, Davy,' she said. 'Wouldn't it be a treat to stay with him for a fortnight? There's the sea, the boats, the beach – and my nephew,

Ham, to play with.'

'But what will my mother do while I'm away?' I asked.

'She's having a holiday too,' Peggotty replied, in a strange voice.

In Yarmouth, Ham was waiting to meet us in front of the inn where the carriage had left us. He was a tall, broad fellow, who carried me on his back down to the sea.

'There's our house, Master Davy,' he said at last.

I looked across the beach, but I could not see any houses. Then I saw a black barge standing on the high ground, with smoke coming from an iron funnel chimney.

'Is that it?' I asked.

'That's it, Master Davy,' he replied.

Inside, the house was beautifully clean and tidy. I had the best bedroom I had ever seen, at the stern of the boat. Mr Peggotty told his niece, Emily, to come to greet me, but she ran away to hide. I later learned that she was an orphan.

As the days passed, we walked around that flat beach at Yarmouth for hours. I fell in love with Emily. As the time came for me to go home, Emily and I cried as we parted. But I was looking forward to seeing my mother again, for she was the greatest comfort in my life. When we arrived, a strange servant opened the door.

'Peggotty!' I cried. 'Where's my mother? Is she dead?'

'No, but I've got something to tell you, Master Davy,' she said. 'You've got a new pa.'

I trembled and turned pale.

Peggotty took me into the best parlour, where Mr Murdstone and my mother were sitting by the fire. She got up to kiss me.

'Clara, control yourself!' Mr Murdstone said.

I ran to my room and cried myself to sleep.

The next six months were very unhappy for me. Mr

Murdstone's sister came to live with us, to take charge of the house. She was gloomy and dark-haired, like her brother – and she disliked me from the first day.

'Ill-mannered boy!' she muttered.

For the time being, I learned my lessons at home with my new father and his sister. How well I could have learned, if it had not been for them. I became sullen and dull-brained because they made me nervous.

One terrible day, Mr Murdstone beat me. I bit his hand. Then he beat me again as if he wanted to beat me to death. I heard my mother and Peggotty crying as he locked me in my bedroom. For five days I stayed there. I saw nobody, except Miss Murdstone. On the fifth night, Peggotty crept to my door.

'Be as quiet as a mouse,' she whispered through the keyhole.

'What is going to happen to me, Peggotty?' I asked. 'Do you know?'

'School. Near London,' she whispered.

'When?' I asked.

'Tomorrow morning,' she whispered back.

CHAPTER TWO

A Great Sadness

It was a long and lonely journey to my new school – Salem House – just outside London. There were no pupils when I arrived because it was still the summer holidays. I had been sent there early as my punishment.

The schoolroom was the bleakest place I had ever seen. In the corner, I caught sight of a placard, on which was written: '*Beware of him. He bites.*'

'Where is the dog?' I asked the master.

'It is for *you* to wear, Copperfield,' he replied sadly. And he tied it to my back at once.

How I suffered, wearing that terrible thing! How I dreaded the boys coming back from their holidays and teasing me about it.

After about a month, Mr Creakle – the Headmaster – returned to school. I was sent to see him. He was a bald, plump man with a fiery red face. He spoke in a whisper as he held me by the ear.

'I have the pleasure of knowing your step-father, Copperfield,' he said. 'Let me tell you one thing. When I says I'll do a thing, I do it.' He let go of my ear.

'Please, sir,' I said. 'May I have this sign taken off before the boys come back…?'

Mr Creakle rose from his chair so angrily that I ran all the way back to my room, where I lay trembling until bedtime.

Tommy Traddles was the first boy to return. I liked him,

for he was kind to me. A boy called J. Steerforth, the head boy, arrived the next day. He was six years older than me and he quickly persuaded me to spend the little money my mother had given me on a midnight feast.

'Mr Creakle has beaten every pupil in the school except me,' Steerforth said. 'Don't worry, young Copperfield, I'll take care of you.'

From that moment, Steerforth was very important in my eyes.

Something else happened during that first half-term which I shall never forget – for it led to a terrible event later in my life. Mr Peggotty and Ham came from Yarmouth to visit me.

I cried to see my old friends, although I tried not to show it. They had brought shrimps and crabs and lobsters for me, and news that my mother and Miss Peggotty were well. They were just beginning to tell me how tall Emily had grown when Steerforth walked by us. I introduced him and he was so charming that Mr Peggotty insisted that I must bring him with me on my next visit to Yarmouth.

We had a great feast that night, although poor Traddles was ill from eating too much crab. The rest of that half-year is a jumble of memories: the frosty mornings, the cold smell of the dark nights, rainy Sundays, the damp smell of boiled food. Then, as the Christmastide holidays came close, I remember the fear in the pit of my stomach: that I would not be allowed to go home.

But I was. What a strange feeling it was to be going to a home that was no longer my home. I went inside with a quiet and timid step, fearing to see Mr Murdstone or his sister. I could hear my mother singing as she used to sing to me, and I found her by the parlour fire, nursing a baby. She kissed me.

'Davy, my pretty boy!' she cried. 'This is your darling new brother.'

We dined with Miss Peggotty by the fireside, for the Murdstones had gone out. I had never been so happy, although my mother's once pretty face now looked tired and anxious. I told them what a fine fellow Steerforth was, and what a strict master Creakle was. I took the baby in my arms and nursed him happily. Then I leaned against my mother as Peggotty darned socks – just as we used to.

It was almost ten o'clock when we heard the sound of carriage wheels. My mother, startled, sent me up to bed at once, for Mr Murdstone thought that children should not stay up late. The next morning, anxious to put matters right, I apologised to Mr Murdstone for biting his hand.

'And how are you, ma'am?' I asked his sister.

She sighed. 'Oh, dear me,' she cried. 'How long are the school holidays?'

It soon became clear that they were not comfortable with me. They hated me holding my baby brother. My poor mother became anxious every time they came into the room where we were. In the evenings, I sometimes sat with Peggotty in the kitchen.

Yet Mr Murdstone and his sister still accused me of being sullen. They forced me to sit with them every evening. I could not move or speak. And so I was not sorry to return to school after a month at home. My mother embraced me as I left. I looked back at her as she held up my brother for me to see.

And so I seemed to lose her.

It was my tenth birthday in March, two months after I returned. I can remember exactly the sort of day it was. Fog and frost hung about the school. The breath of cold boys showed in the spluttering candles. I was summoned from the classroom to go to the parlour. I brightened.

'Mr Peggotty must have sent me a hamper of fish,' I thought.

To my surprise, Mrs Creakle told me to sit on the sofa. 'David,' she said. 'Was your mother well when you left her?' I trembled, but I did not reply. 'I am asking you, because I have to tell you that your poor mama is very ill.' I knew what she would say next. 'She is dead, and so is your little brother,' Mrs Creakle finished.

She was very kind to me, and let me stay in the parlour all day. When I could no longer cry, my grief became a dull ache. I left Salem House the next morning to return home.

Miss Peggotty burst into tears as soon as she saw me. 'Your dear mama was very unhappy, Davy,' she sobbed. 'The last time she was happy was the night you came home from school.'

From that moment, I remembered my mother as I used to know her when she was young. The rest I chose to forget.

CHAPTER THREE

Escape

As soon as my mother's funeral was over, I learned two things from Miss Murdstone: Peggotty had been dismissed from her job and I was not to go back to school. Peggotty decided to return to her brother in Yarmouth and she plucked up the courage to ask if I could go with her for a short while.

'Well, I suppose the boy will be idle anywhere,' Miss Murdstone said. 'And since my brother must not be upset at this unhappy time, I agree.'

Miss Peggotty was sad to leave the house where she had been so happy with my mother. She surprised me by telling me that she was to marry Mr Barkis – the driver of our carriage.

'Then I shall be close to your dear mother's grave,' she said.

Our spirits rose as Ham came to meet us. The houseboat on the beach was as warm and comfortable as before, yet it did not feel the same. I think it was because Emily was not there. She was at school. Later, I strolled along the path to meet her. When she came towards me, I saw that her eyes were bluer and that she had grown more beautiful. She ran away from me, laughing. I was going to kiss her, but she said that she was too old now.

'How's your friend, Steerforth?' Peggotty asked. 'We'd all like to see him, especially Emily.'

Emily blushed and let her curls hide her face.

As the days passed, Emily and I rarely walked on the beach as we used to. She had lessons to learn and jobs to do. She teased me and I felt distant from her. During my stay, Peggotty and Mr Barkis were married.

Then I had to return home.

I was not beaten, I was not starved, but I was neglected. I was not allowed to visit Peggotty, although she visited me or met me close by. Then, one day, I met Mr Murdstone in the lane outside the house. He was with a friend and colleague, a Mr Quinion, who stayed with us that night.

The next morning, Mr Murdstone spoke to me as I was leaving the breakfast table. 'This world is not for moping around as you do, David,' he said. 'It is for action. You are the sort of boy who needs discipline. The sooner you go out to work, the better. So you are going to work for Mr Quinion, my boy. You can earn enough for your food and drink. I shall pay for your lodging. You will leave for London tomorrow, David – and make your way in the world.'

'They want only to be rid of me,' I thought. 'I am only ten years old and they are sending me to hard labour.'

The wine warehouse where I was sent to work stood beside the River Thames in the east of London. Its decaying rooms were filthy and rat-infested. My job, with three other boys, was to empty, wash and label used wine bottles.

No words can describe the unhappiness I felt in that wretched place.

'My hopes of having a distinguished career are in ruins now,' I told myself.

I lodged with the Micawber family. Mr Micawber was friendly, but as shabby as his house. Mrs Micawber was exhausted by her twin babies and her two older children –

and by their lack of money. I became very fond of this family, although their debts weighed on me heavily. I could see no way to help them – or myself.

'There is *nobody* to rescue me from this terrible life,' I told myself.

Ashamed, I told nobody how I felt, not even Miss Peggotty. And even when the Micawbers went to live at the debtor's prison – and I rented a room close to them – my life continued in the same wretched way. At last, Mrs Micawber's family paid their debts and they decided to move to Devon.

Then I was truly alone.

'I cannot bear this life any longer,' I told myself. 'I shall run away from London. I have only one relation left in the whole world and that is my father's aunt, Miss Betsey Trotwood. That is where I shall go. I shall tell *her* my story.'

Dear Peggotty! When I wrote to ask her where my aunt lived, she replied at once, enclosing some money. She told me that Miss Betsey lived in Dover, on the south coast.

I packed my few belongings in a box. How innocent I was in the ways of the world! I paid a boy to carry it to the Dover carriage for me. But he ran off with it – and all my money – and I could not catch him.

There were only three half pence at the bottom of my pocket when I set off along the Dover Road. It was little more than I had brought into the world when my aunt had disappeared from our lives – all because I was a boy.

But would she want me now?

CHAPTER FOUR

My New Life

It took me six days to walk to Dover. On the way, I sold my waistcoat and my jacket to buy bread. My money was soon spent and I had nothing left to sell. I was hungry, thirsty and tired.

By the time I stood in front of my aunt's pretty cottage overlooking the sea, I was a sorry sight. Soon a lady came from the house. She had tied a handkerchief over her hat and she wore gardening gloves.

'Go away!' she cried. 'No boys are allowed here!'

'Please, Aunt... ' I began, certain that it was her, 'I am your nephew, David Copperfield, from Suffolk, where you came the night that I was born. My dear mama has died and I have been very unhappy ever since. I have run away from London and ... ' I burst into tears.

My aunt, who had sat down on the grass in surprise, took me into her parlour. There she gave me something to drink. I cried and cried, until she put me on the sofa with the handkerchief under my dirty feet, crying out, 'Lord help us!'

At last, she called in a gentleman I had seen staring at me from the window. 'Mr Dick,' she said. 'This is my great-nephew, David Copperfield, whom I have often spoken about. I need some good advice. What shall I do with him?'

'Mmm ... let me think,' Mr Dick said. 'Well, I should wash him!'

How that hot bath comforted me! Afterwards, I slept. Then the three of us ate dinner in silence.

'What am I to do with him now, Mr Dick?' my aunt asked at last.

'Well, I should put him to bed,' he replied.

They took me to a bedroom at the top of the house, from where I could see the moonlight on the sea. I looked at the moon's shining path and wished I could see my mother coming down from heaven to me. Then I prayed that my aunt would let me stay and floated into a world of dreams.

When I went down to breakfast the next morning, Miss Betsey told me that she had written to Mr Murdstone.

'Does he know where I am, Aunt?' I asked, alarmed.

She nodded.

'I don't know what I shall do if I have to go back to him!' I cried unhappily.

As we ate dinner that evening, my aunt called out, 'Donkeys!' Through the window, I caught sight of Miss Murdstone sitting on the back of one. Next to her rode Mr Murdstone. They dismounted and entered the parlour.

'I thought it better to answer your letter in person,' Mr Murdstone said, 'however inconvenient the journey has been to reach you.' He glared at me. 'This unhappy boy has been the cause of much trouble to my dear dead wife. My sister and I have tried to cure his vices, but…'

'I believe that he is the worst boy in the world,' Miss Murdstone interrupted.

'Did his mother not leave him any money?' my aunt asked.

'No, it all came to me,' Mr Murdstone replied. 'Now I am here to take David back. From your ... er ... manner, Miss Trotwood, I feel you may be about to help him in his plans to run away. If you do, he can *never* come back to

me. Well, have you anything to say, ma'am?'

'What does the boy think?' my aunt asked. 'Are you ready to go back, David?'

'No, Aunt, and please do not make me,' I begged. 'They have never liked me. They have never been kind to me. I beg you to protect me, for my father's sake.'

My aunt pulled me to her. 'I shall take my chance with the boy, Mr Murdstone,' she said. 'I think I understand what a terrible life his poor mother must have had with you. Oh, yes, you took her in, sir, with your smiling eyes, and your sweet words. And as soon as you had trapped the poor thing, you wore her down. You broke her heart, Mr Murdstone! That is why she died.' She walked them over to the door. 'And if ever I see you on a donkey before my house again, Miss Murdstone, why, I shall knock your bonnet off.'

When they had gone, I kissed Miss Betsey and thanked her. Together, she and Mr Dick consented to be my guardians. She renamed me David Trotwood Copperfield.

And so I began my new life with a new name. Now that the terrible days were over, I felt as if I were in a dream. I have never allowed myself to think of that old life again, for it brings me so much pain.

CHAPTER FIVE

Friends

I became very close to both Miss Betsey and Mr Dick. But I longed to go to school again.

'You can go to school in Canterbury, Trot,' my aunt said, 'and visit me at the weekends. We'll go and see my solicitor, Mr Wickfield. He'll know a good school.'

My aunt drove me in her pony and trap all the way to Canterbury. When we stopped outside Mr Wickfield's old house, I saw a skeleton-like face at the window. It belonged to a boy, with cropped red hair, no eyebrows and no eyelashes. His name was Uriah Heep – and he constantly twisted his body as he rubbed his chin with his long thin hands.

'I have not come for legal advice,' my aunt told her friend. 'I want you to recommend the best school for my great-nephew, Davy. I have adopted him.'

'Why don't you let him lodge here with me for the moment?' Mr Wickfield said kindly. 'He will be no trouble. I can see he is a quiet boy. Then we can find a nearby school for him.'

My aunt agreed. I was introduced to Mr Wickfield's daughter, Agnes, a girl of about my own age. There was a look of great peace and calm on her face. When it was time for my aunt to leave, she embraced me and said, 'Never be mean, Trot, or dishonest or cruel.'

And thus, the next morning, I began my school life once more. My school was close to Canterbury Cathedral and

my master was called Doctor Strong. He was a shabby man, almost as rusty as the railings which surrounded the buildings. I felt strange when I entered the classroom, for it had been a long time since I had been with boys of my own age.

What would they say if they knew that I had scraped and saved and visited the pawnbroker every day to raise money for the Micawber family? They seemed so innocent! They knew nothing of the bad side of London life.

Mr Wickfield was so kind that my uneasiness slowly faded away. And although I still thought of Emily – and loved her – I felt a great peace whenever Agnes was in the room. Dr Strong's school was an excellent one, as different from Mr Creakle's as good is from evil.

I have not mentioned Miss Peggotty since I ran away. Now I wrote a letter to her, enclosing the money she had sent to me. In her reply, she told me sad news: that all the furniture in my old home had been sold and that the house was shut up.

Uriah Heep was not much older than me, but he was too humble, in my opinion. I disliked the way he wrung his hands when he spoke to me. I offered to teach him Latin, to help in his law studies, but he refused. However, he invited me to meet his mother, a widow, who looked exactly like him. As we ate tea, they opened the front door to cool the parlour. To my surprise, Mr Micawber looked in as he passed by, and was invited inside to meet me once more.

Such was the way in which Mr Micawber came back into my life – and befriended Uriah Heep.

The years passed. It was such a happy part of my life! I wore a gold watch and chain. I wore a little ring upon my finger. I fell in love many times. I was sorry to leave school, but I was more than ready to find my own way in the world.

'What occupation do you wish to follow, Trot?' my aunt asked.

'I do not know,' I confessed. 'But it must be something that will not cost you too much money, dear Aunt.'

'A little change might do you good while you decide,' she replied. 'Why don't you visit that woman who lives by the sea, with the strangest of names…?'

'Miss Peggotty?' I asked.

'Yes. I shall send you on this trip alone,' she replied. 'I want you to be a fellow who can stand on his own two feet, Trot. Your mother and father would have been proud to see how you have turned out.'

I called to say farewell to Agnes and her father on my way to Yarmouth. We laughed and teased each other, as we had become accustomed. But she confided that she was worried about her father, for he did not seem well. Uriah Heep was helping more and more with his business.

Passing through London, I bumped into my old school friend, Steerforth! He insisted that I meet his mother before I left for the coast. She was a stern old lady who doted on her only son. But she was not as stern as her companion, Miss Dartle, who had a deep scar on her lip.

'I threw a hammer at her when I was a little boy,' Steerforth confessed.

My dear friend had never visited Yarmouth. He remembered meeting Peggotty and Ham at Salem school, and he asked to come with me. I was delighted to take him and my friends welcomed him warmly. Emily was very shy with Steerforth, but he spoke to her with such charm and respect that she slowly relaxed. Soon she began to talk to me of old times and we laughed once more as we used to.

Peggotty confided in me that he expected her to marry Ham one day.

Steerforth and I stayed in Yarmouth for more than two weeks. I visited my old haunts: the grave of both my parents beneath the tree; my old home, with its wild garden. Steerforth bought a boat, which he named *Emily*. Mr Peggotty agreed to look after it when he returned to London.

Something strange happened the night before I left. For the first time, Emily became very distressed. I had never seen her so before. Her friend, Martha, wanted to go to live in London, but she had not enough money. Ham gave Emily all the money he had saved so that she could give it to her friend.

Emily hid her hands in her face, sobbing. 'Oh, Ham!' she cried, 'I'm not as good a girl as you think I am. My dear, it might be better if you found somebody who's much worthier of you.' She went to kneel at Miss Peggotty's side. 'Oh, dear Aunt, help me!' she cried. 'And Mr David, for the sake of old times, help me too. I *want* to be the wife of a good man. I want to lead a peaceful life, I *do*!'

We soothed her and she slowly calmed. Then she smiled and laughed, ashamed of her tears. I saw her kiss Ham on the cheek.

'I do not understand why she was so distressed last night,' I thought. 'But I shall never tell anyone. Not even my good friend Steerforth.'

Yes, I thought about that night many times, and in the years to come.

CHAPTER SIX

London Life

When I returned to my aunt in Dover, she and I decided that I should start work with a law company in London called Spenlow and Jorkins. She paid a thousand pounds for my training as lawyer's clerk. We travelled to London together, where my aunt rented rooms for me, close to the River Thames.

'Now I am confident, Trot, that the life you lead will make you strong and independent,' she said.

After she had left me to return to Dover, I thought of the bad old days, when I was poor and without friends.

'How happy my life has become,' I said to myself.

I confess that the freedom of my new life went to my head! I met up with Steerforth again and invited him and his friends to dine with me. I had never been so merry and witty as I was that evening – and never had I drunk so much wine. Then we all went to the theatre, where we made a nuisance of ourselves, shouting and laughing and going uninvited into a box full of ladies. One of them turned to look at me, annoyed. It was Agnes, who was staying in London.

'Listen, Trotwood,' she whispered. 'Be quiet, or ask your friends to take you home.'

I did as she suggested. Oh, the shame the next day when I remembered what I had done! And what a terrible headache I suffered! A letter arrived for me from Agnes, inviting me to visit her at her friend's house. I went at once.

Agnes looked so quiet and fresh and good that I shed tears of shame in front of her.

'To think that it was you who saw me behaving so badly, Agnes!' I cried.

'Do not fret, Trot,' she said. 'But I ... I must warn you about Steerforth. He is a bad influence over you. You have made a dangerous friend.' Agnes went on to tell me some unpleasant news: that Uriah Heep wished to become her father's business partner. 'He has seen my father's weaknesses and taken advantage of them,' she said. 'Papa is afraid of him. Oh, Uriah pretends to be humble ... but ... ' She began to cry. 'I beg you, Trotwood, not to turn against Uriah because of what I have told you ... it will make matters worse for Papa ... and for me.'

I saw Uriah Heep later that evening, for Agnes' friend had invited many guests to dine. To my surprise, they included my old school friend, Mr Traddles. We talked of many things, but one thing above all sickened me: Uriah Heep confided in me that he loved Agnes and hoped that she would, in time, return his affection. For one moment, I wanted to pull the red-hot poker from the fire and strike him with it.

But, remembering what Agnes had said, I calmed myself.

The weeks slipped away. After my month's trial as a lawyer's clerk, Mr Spenlow gave me a permanent job. He also invited me to his home to celebrate the return of his daughter, Dora, from her finishing school in Paris.

As soon as I was introduced to her, I fell in love, just like that – in a moment.

But something marred the happiness of that beautiful day. A voice that I knew only too well, announced, 'I know Mr Copperfield.'

It was Dora's friend and travelling companion – Miss Murdstone.

I could not have been more shocked.

'I hope that she will not say anything terrible about me to Dora,' I thought.

After dinner, Miss Murdstone beckoned me to her side. 'David Copperfield,' she said. 'I scarcely recognised you. I do not wish to revive the memory of our past quarrel. Let us meet here as distant acquaintances, not as family. Are you agreed?'

'You and your brother treated me and my mother cruelly,' I said, 'and I shall believe that as long as I live. But I shall say no more on the matter.'

A few weeks later, Steerforth brought me a letter from Miss Peggotty.

'Why did *you* bring this letter?' I asked him, surprised.

'Oh, I have been sailing in Yarmouth this past week,' he replied.

I read the letter. 'Mr Barkis is very ill,' I told him. 'I shall go to Yarmouth first thing in the morning.'

'Will you spend one last night at my house, my dear friend?' Steerforth asked.

Puzzled, I agreed. Before I went to bed, he said, 'Davy, if anything should ever separate us, you must think of me when I was at my best, old boy.'

'You have no best or worst, dear friend,' I replied.

I looked into Steerforth's bedroom before I left early the next morning. He was sleeping soundly with his head on his arms, as I had often seen him at school.

'What strange words he spoke last night', I thought. 'What did he mean?'

CHAPTER SEVEN

Scandal

I arrived in Yarmouth just before poor Mr Barkis died. The night of his funeral – the night before I returned to London – the most terrible thing happened. Now, as I write about it, a deep dread comes over me.

I was visiting Peggotty at his house on the beach. It was raining heavily and we were waiting for Ham and Emily to arrive. At last, Ham came in alone, drenched to the skin and deadly pale. He asked me to step outside. He stood in the pouring rain, weeping and crying, 'Oh ... oh, Master Davy ... '

'Ham! My poor dear fellow!' I cried. 'Tell me what's wrong.'

'She's gone!' he cried. 'Emily's run away and I wish that God would kill her before she's disgraced. How am I going to tell Peggotty?'

It was too late, for Peggotty stood in the doorway. I shall never forget the look on his face, not if I live for five hundred years. He held out a piece of paper to me. 'Read it, sir,' he said in a quivering voice, 'but slow, so as I can understand.'

We went inside. In the midst of a deadly silence, I read the following: *"When you, who love me so much better than I ever deserved, see this, I shall be far away."* The letter was dated the night before. *"I shall never come back unless he makes me a lady. I love you all. God bless you all. My last tears and love are for my dear uncle Peggotty.*

Emily."

'Who's the man she's gone with?' Peggotty asked.

'Go outside, Master Davy,' Ham said. 'You shouldn't hear this.'

But I sat down, shocked. I felt Peggotty's arm clasped around my shoulder.

'It ain't no fault of yours, Master Davy,' Ham said, 'but his name's Steerforth – and he's a villain.'

Mr Peggotty put on his hat and coat and made for the door. 'I'm going to find her!' he cried. 'I'll find her wherever she is in her shame and bring her back here.'

We prevented him from leaving. And when he started to cry, I cried with him.

'I shall never see Steerforth again,' I thought. 'Yet never has a friend been so dear to me.'

Mr Peggotty returned to London with me, for he was determined to speak to Steerforth's mother. She welcomed us kindly and read Emily's letter.

'I just want to know one thing, ma'am,' Peggotty said. 'Will your son marry my niece?'

'No,' Mrs Steerforth replied. 'It would be impossible, since she is a poor and ignorant girl.'

'You don't know what it's like to lose your child, ma'am,' he said. 'I do. But we'll never be ashamed of her. One day, we'll all be equal before God.'

Mrs Steerforth's face softened for a moment. Then she became angry. 'My son has deserted me for this wretched girl,' she cried. 'He has forgotten all family honour and his duty towards me. If he does not rid himself of her, he shall never enter my house again.'

We left. And Mr Peggotty, a broken man, set off in search of Emily: in London and in Europe, anywhere where he thought Steerforth might have taken her.

It was Dora who brought happiness back into my life after the loss of my dear friends. The more I despaired of them, the more my love for her grew. We became secretly engaged whilst Miss Murdstone was away, attending her brother's marriage. I wrote to tell Agnes of my great happiness, but I did not tell her about Steerforth – only that Emily had run away from Yarmouth. I knew that she would guess the truth.

Miss Peggotty came to stay with me in London while I helped to settle her financial affairs. One day, returning from my office, I was surprised to see that my door was wide open. Inside, I found my aunt and Mr Dick sitting on a pile of bags and belongings.

'I know my aunt well,' I thought. 'She would not have come here unless she had something important to tell me.'

'Why do you think I am here, Trot?' she asked.

'I cannot guess, Aunt,' I replied.

'I am ruined!' she cried. 'I have lost every penny that I ever invested with my dear friend Spenlow, except for my cottage, which I have had to rent out.'

Shock silenced me. The next morning, I asked Mr Spenlow if my aunt's money – a thousand pounds – could be returned to her. But it was not possible. To make matters worse, Miss Murdstone returned and found out about Dora's engagement. She told her father at once and he forbade me to see her again. This was not the end of those bad times. Not long afterwards, Mr Spenlow died in an accident and Dora was left with very little money.

'I dread being poor again more than anything,' I said to myself. 'How can I ever forget those hard times when I was a boy? How can I ever marry Dora now?'

CHAPTER EIGHT

Dear Dora

It was dear Agnes who came to my rescue. She told me that my old schoolmaster, Dr Strong, was looking for somebody to help him to compile a new dictionary. We agreed that I would work for him early mornings and evenings. I was worn out with it all and thought I saw the first grey hairs on my head.

'Do you have to work *so* hard, Doady?' Dora cried.

'But what shall we live on without work?' I asked her.

I confided my worries only to Agnes, when I visited her and her father in Canterbury. 'Dora is a timid little thing, Agnes, and easily frightened, although she likes you very much.'

'You should not depend upon me, Trotwood,' she replied. 'You should depend upon Dora.'

I kissed her hand. 'Whenever I come to you, Agnes, I feel such peace and rest.'

Agnes had her own worries. Uriah Heep was now her father's business partner and he and his mother had moved into their house. In the time that I spent there, I was scarcely alone with Agnes and her father. Uriah even followed me when I went out to walk.

'I came out to be alone,' I told him coldly.

Uriah raised his big hands until they touched his chin and rubbed them together. 'You're quite a dangerous rival, Mr Copperfield,' he said, 'and you always was, you know.'

'I am engaged to another young lady,' I cried. 'I hope that satisfies you.' He caught hold of my hand and squeezed it with his damp, fishy fingers. 'And may I tell you that Miss Agnes Wickfield is as far out of your reach as the moon is from the earth!' I cried.

'I've eaten humble pie all my life, David Copperfield,' he replied. 'But now I've got a little power.'

I looked at his mean face in the moonlight and we did not speak again all the way back to the house. But, at dinner, Uriah Heep made a fool of himself once more. He raised his glass and shouted, 'I adore Agnes Wickfield and I wish to be her husband!'

Mr Wickfield rose from the table with a cry. He tore at his hair as I held him, until Agnes came to take him to his room. Later, she came to say goodbye to me, for I was to leave early in the morning. I could see that she had been weeping.

'Tell me that you will not sacrifice yourself to that man for the sake of your father,' I cried.

She smiled as she always did, and told me not to worry.

Let me now pause as I remember this important time of my life. I was twenty-one years old and in employment – and in secret, I had begun to write short stories which had been published in a magazine. I had bought a cottage in Highgate Village, north of London, for I was to be married to Dora. Miss Peggotty came from Yarmouth to make herself useful, cleaning and scrubbing our little home in readiness for our marriage.

Sometimes I passed Mr Peggotty in the dark streets of London, still searching for Emily, but I did not speak to him at such times. He was so lost in his thoughts.

I married dear Dora, with all my good friends to wish me well. Although I loved my wife deeply, I soon came to realise that I had to shoulder all the cares of life. My sweet and childish wife was afraid of the servants and she was afraid of

my aunt. She only wanted to play with her beloved dog, Jip.

One evening, about a year after I married, I was returning from a walk and thinking about the new book I was then writing. I passed by Mrs Steerforth's house. I often did, but I always hurried past without a glance. But this time, a servant-girl asked me if I would go inside and speak to Miss Dartle. I agreed, reluctantly.

Miss Dartle was thinner and paler than before. 'Has the girl been found?' she asked.

'Emily? No,' I replied. 'Why do you wish to know?'

'She has run away from him!' she cried.

'Run away?' I repeated.

'Yes, he ... he finished their friendship in Italy and when he had left to sail to Spain, she ran away. Perhaps she is dead,' Miss Dartle replied, with the cruellest look I have ever seen on a face.

I thought it only right to tell Mr Peggotty at once. I found him at the room he kept for his visits to London. He wept when I told him.

'I'm sure that my sweet Emily's alive,' he cried. 'She won't dare go to Yarmouth, but she might come here, to London.'

'If she does, she will look for her friend, Martha,' I said.

He shivered. 'I've seen that poor girl in the streets,' he said. 'I think I know where to look.'

'Then let us go together,' I replied.

We found Martha in the filthiest and most dreadful part of London. When we approached her, and told her who we were, I had never heard such despair in a human voice. 'Emily was a good friend to me,' she wept. 'I wouldn't wish her to live such a terrible life as mine. If I find her, I'll bring her to you, I promise.'

CHAPTER NINE

Unhappy Days

The unhappy feelings that I used to have as a child came back to me. I did not know where they came from. I loved Dora and I had some success with my writing. Yet my happiness was not complete.

'I wish that Dora could help me more,' I thought. 'I wish that she were not so childish.'

During the second year of our marriage, Dora did not seem so strong. She tired easily. She still looked very pretty, but she rested more and more. My aunt became the best nurse there was.

My good friends were a great support to me. I saw Mr Traddles often, as well as my aunt and Mr Dick. I had news from Canterbury of Agnes and her father – and to my surprise, of Mr Micawber, who now worked as a clerk to Uriah Heep.

It was some months since I had found Martha in London and I had heard nothing from her. One evening, I was walking alone in my garden when I saw her, lurking in the shadows.

'I knows where Emily is,' she whispered. 'I've been to see Peggotty, but he ain't there. I wrote down where he's to come.'

I went with her at once. We took a carriage to a tall dirty house in a shabby London street. As we reached the top of its broken staircase, I saw Miss Dartle enter one of the rooms. I could not believe my eyes. We could hear her harsh and cruel voice and the gentle voice of Emily in reply.

'We must wait for Peggotty,' I whispered. 'Emily would be ashamed to see me.'

Just as we felt that we could endure Emily's distress no longer, Mr Peggotty arrived. Miss Dartle slipped quickly into the shadow of the stairs. My poor dear Emily! She cried out, 'Uncle!' and fainted in his arms.

Enormous events now came to shake our quiet lives. Mr Peggotty talked of sailing to Australia with Emily, where nobody would know of her shame. Then Mr Micawber, in a great outburst of anger, confessed to my aunt and I that Uriah Heep had forged Mr Wickfield's signature on many documents. In this way, he had made money by committing fraud, as well as getting his hands on my aunt's money.

I loathed Uriah Heep more than I had ever done, but I was pleased that he would no longer be part of our lives – especially Agnes'. My aunt, thankful that Mr Micawber had dared to speak out against Uriah, offered to lend him some of her recovered money so that he could start his new life in Australia.

My dear Dora weakened more each day. She did not come downstairs any more, but lay in bed all day with Jip in her arms. My aunt nursed her faithfully. Dora begged me to send for Agnes and she came from Canterbury at once. As they talked upstairs, I sat by the fire with Jip.

Suddenly, I saw that he was no longer breathing. And as I wept for the poor old dog, Agnes came downstairs, weeping too, and pointing to heaven.

It was over. My dear Dora was dead.

As I sat with Jip before the fire, darkness came over me and, for some time, everything was blotted from my mind.

Then, slowly, I sank under the load of my sorrow.

'Why don't you travel abroad, Trotwood?' Agnes said. 'It will help to lift your spirits.'

I agreed.

I now approach an event in my life so awful that I have seen it looming even since I picked up this pen to write. I dreamed of it for years afterwards, whenever a storm blew up.

CHAPTER TEN

The Storm

As the time rapidly approached for me to sail for Europe, I decided to visit Yarmouth.

'I can see Ham and help to make the final arrangements for Mr Peggotty's long journey to Australia,' I thought.

It was a stormy September day when I left London. As darkness fell, the gusts of wind and rain became so strong that we feared that the coach might overturn. We came at last to Yarmouth. Long before we saw the sea, we saw the waves on the horizon, as tall as towers. The town was full of people in the streets, fearing their chimneys would blow down. On the beach, women wailed for their husbands still out fishing. Old sailors shook their heads as they looked up at the sky.

The noise of the surging sea terrified me. Ham was not on the beach, nor at his house.

I hardly tasted my dinner at the inn. My unease grew. I walked up and down, glancing at the clock. I could not sleep, but lay listening to that terrible wind. Eventually I fell into the depths of sleep. The next morning, I awoke to the sound of cannon being fired, and the cry from below: 'Shipwreck!'

I dressed quickly and we all ran down to the sea. The swell of the sea was even more terrifying. Peggotty's barge was smashed to pieces. From the beach, we watched a ship break up on the rocks. Its sailors plunged into the water. Only one man remained, clinging to the broken mast.

Then I saw Ham on the beach, winding a rope around his waist. I held him back, but he pushed me away. Then he made for the wreck. He was so near, but the power of the wind and the waves made it dangerous. With one more stroke, Ham could have reached the man on the mast. But a vast wall of water took the ship away – and Ham with it.

They hauled him in at my feet – dead.

Soon after, the body of the man clinging to the mast was washed ashore. On the part of the beach where Emily and I used to gather shells – among the ruins of the house he had so badly wronged – lay Steerforth, his head upon his arms as I had often seen him lie at school. Never had he seemed so dear to me as then.

The time came to wave farewell to Mr Peggotty and Emily – and Martha. The Micawber family were sailing on that fine ship too. Then it was my turn to leave England. Yet the despair that I felt deepened. I had left everybody that I loved. I thought of those who had died, and the house I had loved as a child now broken by the sea.

With this darkening cloud over my head, I travelled for many months through Europe. I was always restless, moving from place to place; but sometimes I lingered, although I had no reason to do so. One day, I was walking in the Swiss Alps. At sunset, I was coming down to the valley when I paused to look back at the sun shining on the snow above me. It was so beautiful that I cried for the first time since Dora had died.

I also received my first letter from Agnes that same day.

"I am happy and well," she wrote. *"I have started a small school at home and it is going well. Now, dear Trot, you must stay away from England until you are well. Sorrow is not a sickness, but a strength, and you will be better for it in the end.*

I am always with you in my thoughts, and send you my sisterly affection.

Agnes."

Home became very dear to me as I read her letter – and so did she.

'But I have left it too late,' I thought. 'She is like a sister to me now. I can never tell her that I love her.'

I stayed away from England for three years. During that time, I took exercise and fresh air, and I grew stronger. I wrote a novel too, which Traddles had published for me.

At last, I decided to return. I landed in England once

more on a wintry autumn evening. Traddles, newly married, welcomed me warmly. Then I set off for Dover to see my aunt and we talked long into the night.

'When shall you ride to Canterbury to see Agnes?' she asked. 'You will find her father greatly changed. But she is as good and as beautiful as ever. She could have married many times ... but I suspect that she is already in love, Trot.'

I visited Agnes the next day and many times during the next two months.

'Do you know any more of ... of the man Agnes loves?' I asked my aunt.

'No,' she replied, 'but I think she will marry soon.'

I rode at once to see Agnes. How well I remember that wintry ride! The wind blew ice into my face and the horse's hooves clattered hard. I found her alone. Her pupils had returned home and she was reading by the fire. She welcomed me and sat in one of the old-fashioned windows as we talked.

'Agnes, shall I tell you what I came to say?' I asked. 'I have learned that ... you are in love. Tell me who it is, dear Agnes! Let me be your friend, as you have been mine.'

Agnes hurried from the window, put her hands to her face and burst into tears. 'Don't speak to me now,' she cried.

'What have I done?' I asked. I caught hold of her around the waist. 'Dear Agnes, even when I loved Dora, I was incomplete without you. When I lost her, how would I have survived without you? I went away, loving you, Agnes and I have returned home, loving you.'

Agnes cried again. Then she laughed and said, 'I have loved you all my life, dear Trot.'

My aunt was right. We were married within a fortnight.

My story is almost finished. Yet there is one more thing I must tell you.

I had been married for ten happy years, and had become quite well known as a novelist. Agnes and I were sitting by the fire one spring evening, and three of our children were playing close by. The servant told me that a stranger wished to see me, an old friend.

It was Mr Peggotty! He had returned from Australia briefly to visit Miss Peggotty.

He was an old man now, but he was still in good health. He sat before our fire with my children on his knee.

'Why, Master Davy,' he said, 'you were only as big as these little ones when I first set eyes on you. And Emily weren't no bigger.'

When the children had gone to bed, he sat between Agnes and myself. 'Tell me everything,' I said. I began to listen to his old, familiar voice.

'Well, we've thrived, Master Davy. We've worked hard, but we've not lacked for anything.'

'And how is Emily?' Agnes and I asked together.

'She heard nothing of that fellow's death, not until a traveller from Suffolk passed through and told us. She was low for a long time. I wonder if you would know her now, Master Davy. Her blue eyes are sorrowful, and she's still timid. She never married, but she does some teaching and the children love her.' As we talked by the fire, I thought of those innocent days when we were young together.

Before Peggotty sailed back, we went to Yarmouth together, and we talked of many friends on the journey: Martha, who had married, and Mr Micawber, who was a magistrate. In the little churchyard, we knelt at Ham's grave. There Peggotty lifted a handful of soil.

'For Emily, Master Davy,' he said. 'I promised her.'

Now my story *is* finished. And I thank God that I am the happiest man alive.